YOU GOT ALIEN TROUBLE!
A SEVEN BRIDES FOR SEVEN ALIEN BROTHERS STORY

HONEY PHILLIPS

Copyright © 2023 by Honey Phillips

All rights reserved. No part of this book may be used or reproduced by any means, graphic, electronic, or mechanical, including photocopying, recording, taping or by any information storage retrieval system without the written permission of the author.

Disclaimer

This book is a work of fiction. Names, characters, places, and incidents are products of the author's imagination or are used fictitiously and are not to be construed as real. Any resemblance to actual events, locales, organizations, or people, living or dead, is entirely coincidental.

Edited by Lindsay York at LY Publishing Services

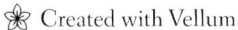 Created with Vellum

CHAPTER 1

Rosie knew something was wrong as soon as she entered the barn. Petunia, her milking cow, was huddled against the rear of her stall rather than coming to meet her as she usually did. The chickens clucked nervously from within their coop, and an icy finger trailed down Rosie's spine.

Dammit. What had that bastard Matthew done now?

Matthew Johnson owned the largest farm in their cluster. Of the sixteen original families only three remained, and he was determined to get his hands on all three of their farms. If a winning smile and a lowball offer didn't work, he turned to threats and sabotage. The Thompsons had been forced to sell after their creek mysteriously dried up, and the Garcias after they found most of the chicken flock slaughtered by unknown predators. *Predators, my ass.* Johnson's ruffians hadn't even bothered to disguise the knife marks when they slit the chickens' throats.

He hadn't yet resorted to sabotage with her, although his visits were becoming increasingly threatening. She straightened her shoulders—whatever he had done, it was best to deal with it now.

She tried to adjust the lighting but the limited amount of power remaining in the solar batteries meant the overhead lights weren't bright enough to chase away all the shadows. With her hand on the holster of her gun she made her way quietly down the corridor between the empty stalls. Her three remaining horses preferred to stay outside until winter arrived. The stalls to the left were empty as well, except for Petunia and her heifer. Now that she was running the farm by herself, she'd had to sell the rest of the dairy cows at auction.

The cows weren't really cows, of course, and neither were the chickens or the horses. All of the farm animals on Cresca were hybrid versions of the original Earth animals, but Rosie had grown up on this planet and they were all she'd ever known.

Other than her thudding heart, she didn't hear any indication that anything was wrong until she was almost to the last stall on the left. A low groan, the sound tormented enough that she winced in sympathy before tightening her grip on her gun. What the hell was Matthew up to?

Peeking cautiously around the edge of the stall, she didn't see anything at first. The floor was still covered with a thick layer of unused straw, old and musty by now, and it took a moment for her to realize that the lump against the back wall was not the result of the wind pushing the straw around. Instead, it mostly concealed the fact that a figure was lying there—a very large figure. As her eyes adjusted to the dimness, she picked out the boots pressed against one side of the stall, the kind of scuffed, metallic boots worn by spaceport workers, not the surrounding farmers. Once she recognized the boots, it was easier to see the rest of the huge body filling the back of the stall. If his boots were on one side and his head on the other, the stranger had to be over seven feet tall.

He moaned again. Her hand still tight on her gun, she walked cautiously into the stall, then nudged one of his boots with her more practical rubber one.

"You all right, mister?"

No response, so she nudged a little harder.

"Hey! Do you need help?"

This time he responded, sitting up with incredible speed as she jumped back with a muffled squeak. Before she could raise her gun, he collapsed down into the straw, landing on his back this time.

Oh, crap. Not a man at all.

Now she could see the emerald highlights in the dark hair that flopped across his face. His features were similar to those of a man but stronger and more angular, and his skin was a pale minty green. She'd had a brief glimpse of glittering silver eyes before his eyelids fluttered shut.

An alien. What the hell is an alien doing in my barn?

On the positive side, she was quite sure he wasn't working for Matthew. On more than one occasion she'd heard Matthew ranting about the presence of those damn aliens on *his* planet. He didn't seem to appreciate the irony that humans were also aliens on Cresca. But the human settlers tended to keep to themselves and they rarely encountered other species.

Or at least not until seven years ago when a small group of alien warriors purchased an isolated ranch in the mountains behind Wainwright, the closest town. Their presence had disturbed many of the residents, especially when each of the aliens had found human brides during the long winter five years ago. Since then, the aliens had worked with the town and built up a thriving trading business. But while the townspeople might grudgingly accept them, in the more remote areas, prejudice still lingered.

If Matthew didn't hire him, what is he doing here?

Had he been headed for the ranch? If so, he was a long way off course. And what was wrong with him? Was he wounded?

Most of the straw had fallen away from his body during his abortive attempt to move, and she did a quick check for any obvious signs of injury. He was wearing a dark jumpsuit, the kind worn by those who worked on spaceships. It was stained and faded but despite its bedraggled state, she didn't see any rips in the fabric or anything that looked like blood. Biting her lip, she put her gun back in her holster and knelt down next to him, uneasily aware of his enormous size as she got closer. Tentatively, she reached for his hand, then immediately dropped it.

Damn, he was hot—his skin like hot coals beneath her fingers. It might be natural for his species, but given his moans, she suspected he was running a fever. Very cautiously she put her hand over his heart, or at least what she thought his heart would be. His heart thumped steadily beneath her hand, a little fast perhaps but reassuringly strong. Now that she was next to him, she could see the wedge of skin in the open neck of his jumpsuit and the dark, angry-looking tracery of his veins. They also might have been natural, but they didn't look right to her. Could he have been poisoned?

He obviously needed help, but what could she do? There was a doctor in Wainwright, but that was a good day's journey away and she couldn't leave the farm unprotected for that long. In previous years she would have turned to Mrs. Miller for assistance, but the healer's family had been one of the first that Matthew ran off.

She was still trying to come up with a plan when a burning hot hand covered hers, still resting over his heart. Startled, she jumped and looked up at his face. Those glittering silver eyes were open again.

"Mine," he growled.

Before she could respond, he pulled her down into the straw and rolled on top of her, his huge, scorching body covering hers. She opened her mouth to protest and his mouth closed over hers. A hot, rough tongue stroked into her mouth with unerring precision, tasting like fire and spice.

How long had it been since she'd been touched, let alone kissed? For one brief second she gave into that heated, seductive touch, but then she felt the thick ridge of his erection between her legs despite the fabric separating them, and she panicked. She tried to reach for her gun, but it was wedged under the heavy weight of his body. Knowing that it wouldn't do any good, she pummeled his shoulders with her fists, then in a last fit of desperation, she bit his tongue.

CHAPTER 2

Harkan was so lost in the sweetness of his female's mouth that it took him far too long to realize that she was struggling rather than responding. Just as he was about to draw back, her small teeth clamped down on his tongue, surprisingly sharp despite their size, and he roared as his blood filled his mouth. He lifted his head and gave her a shocked look.

"Why did you do that?"

"I didn't say you could kiss me," she said indignantly, blue eyes sparkling.

Her pretty face was flushed, pink tinting the soft gold of her skin. The brown hair that had been pulled back so tightly was now curling wildly around her face. *Human*, he noted absently, but it didn't matter.

"But you are mine," he protested.

His head felt swollen, his thoughts dizzy and unfocused, but he was absolutely sure about that fact.

"No, I'm not."

She wiggled beneath him, her soft curves rubbing deliciously against his body and tormenting his aching cock. How long had it been since he'd had an erection? Even before the sickness... *The sickness.* The words triggered something in his confused mind, but before he could capture it, she wiggled again and he finally realized she was trying to escape.

His body didn't want to respond but calling on his last reserves of strength, he managed to roll to one side. She immediately slipped free, leaving him feeling cold and alone despite the heat burning through his veins. She put her hand on her weapon as she glared at him, and he nodded approvingly. His fierce little mate.

"Where... where am I?"

"In my barn," she said, pretty lips pursed. "Why are you here?"

He searched for an answer but all he found was a confused blur, and he shook his head.

"Were you going to Wainwright? Or the ranch?"

Something flickered at the word *ranch*, but it was gone just as quickly and he shook his head again. She sighed.

"Do you at least know that you're on Cresca?"

"Not on Vizal?"

"Vizal? Is that your home?"

"Yes."

The answer came automatically, but it was accompanied by an overwhelming wave of sadness he didn't understand. She hesitated, then crouched down a short distance away. He suspected she was trying to stay out of reach. He could have reached her easily, but although he wanted her back in his arms, he didn't want to frighten her.

"Is that when you were injured? During the war on Vizal?" She shook her head. "No, of course not. The war was over seven years ago."

He flinched and her gaze sharpened. "What is it? Did you remember something?"

"W-war," he stuttered.

Images flashed in his head—horrible, painful images—and his vision blurred. Darkness roared over him, pulling him back down into the shadows even as he tried to reach for her.

The next time he awoke she was gone, and an anguished howl escaped his lips. Had she just been a dream, an illusion brought on by fever and sickness? A hint of sweetness floated through the air, distracting him, and then she was there. His pretty little mate bending anxiously over him. He hadn't dreamed her after all, and he sagged back against the straw in relief.

"What's wrong? I mean, other than whatever is already wrong with you?"

"You're back," he said, and reached for her hand.

She hesitated for a long moment and then very lightly placed her fingers over his.

"No trying to pull me down," she said, patting the holster of her adorable little weapon.

"I apologize, my mate. I did not mean to alarm you."

She sighed, but her fingers squeezed his for a brief second before she moved away.

"I'm not your mate."

He bit back his immediate protest. His mind might not be clear on many things, but he was quite certain about that one. *A patient hunter reaps the reward*, he reminded himself.

"What is your name, my... friend?"

"Friend, hmm? I suppose that will do. My name is Rosalie Mackenzie, but everyone calls me Rosie."

"Rosalie? A sweet name for a sweet ma—female," he amended quickly. "I am Harkan. I am honored to meet you."

She gave him a suspicious look.

"Aren't you a sweet talker all of a sudden? Guess all the fluids I've been pouring down your throat must have helped. You seem better, and the outline of your veins has faded."

"I feel somewhat restored," he agreed and managed to sit up.

As he did, the top half of his jumpsuit fell down to his waist. Rosalie's cheeks turned a pretty shade of pink.

"You spilled almost as much as you swallowed," she muttered. "I had to clean you up."

"I do not object. You may do whatever you wish with me."

"What I wish to do is to get you out of the barn and into the house. Do you think you can stand?"

He contemplated the question. He did not wish to admit weakness in front of his female, but even moving to a sitting position had taxed his strength.

"Perhaps. Although you may have to assist me," he added reluctantly.

She took a step towards him, then paused and gave him a stern look.

"This isn't a trap, is it? Remember that I'm armed."

She patted the holster of her weapon, and he nodded approvingly.

"My fierce little mate. I mean, friend," he added hastily.

She shook her head again, but he saw her pretty lips twitch.

"All right, but you'd better behave yourself."

She bent down and put his arm over her shoulders while she slid her other arm around his waist. Her closeness had the inevitable effect on his body, but he did his best to ignore it as he tried to wrestle himself into a standing position. Despite her small size, she was surprisingly strong and managed to provide enough support that he could stagger to his feet.

As soon as he was upright, she took a step back. The unfastened jumpsuit that had been pinned between them immediately slid down to his feet, leaving him completely naked and ferociously erect.

CHAPTER 3

*R*osie knew that her mouth had dropped open, knew that she was staring, but she couldn't look away. The only other cock she had seen was her deceased husband's and it hadn't even been half the size. Harkan's was not only much longer, but wider as well. A ladder of thick ridges ran up the underside, clearly visible since his erection was pointing up towards his stomach. *What do they feel like*, she wondered, her fingers twitching with the urge to touch him.

His cock jerked under her fascinated gaze, and she jumped as he gave a muffled groan.

"You are testing my control, little mate."

Too embarrassed to argue with the term, she quickly reached down to grasp his jumpsuit and pull it back into place. He moved at the same time, and for the briefest second the velvety hardness of his cock brushed against her cheek. The urge to explore him was even stronger this time, but she yanked the jumpsuit up his legs instead. He winced when the fabric collided with his balls, but he grasped the material, and she quickly turned away.

"Can you manage?" she asked.

Damn. Even though she'd tried to sound calm, her voice came out breathless and husky.

"Yes."

At least he sounded just as strained.

"I'll wait outside until you're dressed."

She fled out into the passage, then leaned against the nearest stall, her hands shaking. *What in the world is wrong with me?* She'd never been particularly interested in the opposite sex—or they in her, to be honest. Her marriage had been based on necessity rather than love. She'd done her best to be a dutiful wife, although she found the whole process awkward and embarrassing. Hector had been equally unenthusiastic, but he had also done his duty, hoping that she would give birth to an heir for the farm.

Those brief weekly couplings had never aroused her the way her alien did. Ever since that first kiss something had changed—she was aware of her body in a way she had never been before. Aware of the heaviness of her breasts and the tingling peaks of her nipples, the low, pulsing ache between her thighs. Even when she'd been supporting his head and trying to get liquid down his throat, she'd been conscious of the strong muscles beneath the smooth, hot skin. She'd even been tempted to take a peek at the bulge that appeared beneath his jumpsuit every time she tended to him, but she'd forced herself to refrain.

Perhaps if she had peeked, she wouldn't have been quite so shocked.

That's all it is, she told herself firmly. *Shock. It's just because he's so different.*

But then he appeared next to her, big and imposing even though his knees were trembling, and her heart skipped a beat. Doing her best to hide her reaction, she gave him a bright, false smile.

"I think you're getting better. The discoloration on your veins is fading."

"Veins?"

He swayed. She swore and put her arm around his waist to steady him, carefully ignoring the fact that it felt so right to be there.

"Maybe I spoke too soon."

"I just had a memory, or at least I think it was a memory."

He shook his head in obvious frustration.

"I'm sure it will come back to you," she said soothingly. "But let's try and get you back to the house before you collapse."

"I'm quite capable of standing," he said stiffly, but she could feel his body shaking.

"Good. Then this won't take long."

Her optimism proved unfounded. They had to stop in the breezeway between the barn and the carriage house. She let him lean against the wall while she tried to shrug some feeling back into her shoulders.

The final journey through the garden, up the steps to the porch, and into the house seemed to last forever. She could feel his body trembling even though he never complained, and her shoulders ached from trying to support his weight. Together they managed to stagger through the door. As soon as they were inside, she guided him into the parlor she'd converted into a bedroom and pushed him gently down onto the bed.

His arm was still wrapped around her shoulders, and he collapsed so rapidly that she went with him, ending up sprawled across that huge, hot body.

"Here we are again," she sighed.

She knew she should get up, but he felt so good beneath her, big and hard and reassuring. His other arm came up to wrap around her waist, and she felt surprisingly safe, despite the massive ridge of his erection throbbing between her legs.

For a long moment they lay together in silence, the morning sunlight flooding in through the big windows and only the sound of the birds in the orchard disturbing the quiet. She'd spent most of the past twenty-four hours trying to care for him and keep up with her chores. Exhaustion washed over her, and she was almost asleep when she felt his hands stroking her hair. He gently freed the long strands from her usual tight braid.

"Your hair is so soft. Like silk between my fingers." His voice lowered to a deep growl. "But I believe your lips were softer. May I taste them again?"

I shouldn't. I really shouldn't.

She opened her mouth to tell him no.

"Yes," she whispered instead.

He immediately pulled her up his body, her breasts rubbing deliciously against the hard planes of his chest, until her face was level with his. Silver eyes glittered up at her and she could see the hunger in them, but all he did was smooth her disheveled curls back from her face.

"My pretty little mate," he murmured, and she had the sudden urge to cry.

No one had ever called her pretty, or little for that matter. She had the sturdy body of her pa's side of the family—good breeding stock, he'd told her once. He might even have meant it as a compliment.

She started to protest, but before she could say anything he gently tugged her head down and pressed his mouth against hers. She expected him to kiss her with the same fiery intensity he had shown before, but instead he sipped delicately at her lips, tasting, teasing, until she was the one who wanted more, shyly slipping her tongue between his lips. She felt him tense, felt his cock throb beneath her, but even then he held back, letting her explore.

He tasted as hot and delicious as she remembered, and this time she noticed the ridges running down the center of his tongue, ridges that mimicked the ones on his cock. What would they feel like on other parts of her body? Her nipples stiffened even more at the thought of him kissing her breasts or even... lower.

She had never experienced such a thing, but before her best friend Mary's family had sold their farm to Matthew, Mary had told her about the acts that could be performed between a man or woman—acts she had certainly never encountered in her married life. Her nipples throbbed, and she tried to rub them against his chest to relieve the lingering ache.

He growled again, the sound reverberating deliciously through their tightly pressed bodies as his hand slipped down from her waist to her ass. His hand tightened on the generous flesh as he began slowly rocking her back and forth across his cock. She tried to move faster, chasing that elusive pleasure, but he continued his slow, unhurried rhythm, matching it to his kisses—long, drugging kisses that filled her senses and left her clinging to him as her body tightened, perched on the edge of a cliff. She started to panic, the intensity of the sensation scaring her,

"You're safe, my sweet mate," he murmured soothingly against her mouth, his hand stroking her head.

With a tiny sigh, she relaxed against him. He started rocking her again. and this time she gave herself over to the sensations rushing through her body and the sweet intensity of his kisses. He pulled her tighter against his body, his thick cock pressing directly against the swollen nub of flesh between her thighs, and with a shuddering gasp she flew over the edge. A tidal wave of pleasure swept over her, leaving her limp and dazed in his arms.

"Good girl," he whispered.

She buried her face against his neck, suddenly feeling shy as he murmured words of praise and gently stroked her hair. She could feel his heart beating against her chest, the steady rhythm filling her head. He was still erect, and she raised her head, not quite sure what to say. As she did she realized that she hadn't just heard his heart beating. Hoofbeats were coming down the drive. He must have heard them as well because his body tensed. He sat up with that astonishing speed, placing her next to him as he did, his face grim and fierce.

"Someone is coming."

"I know," she sighed as she rose to her feet. Unfortunately, the only person likely to be visiting her was Matthew.

CHAPTER 4

Harkan knew from his mate's reaction that the approaching visitor was unwelcome. A moment ago she had been soft and happy in his arms. Now she was frowning, her small shoulders tense and her blunt little teeth worrying the soft curve of her lower lip, still swollen from his kisses. Whoever was coming needed to leave. Immediately.

He started to rise to his feet, then swayed, his knees giving out and sending him back down on the bed. *Fuck.* What had happened to him—what was still happening? His thoughts were a muddled blur, brief flashes of memory appearing and then disappearing.

"What are you trying to do?" she demanded. "You barely made it into the house. Just stay where you are."

"I will not leave you alone to deal with a threat," he insisted, hoping that his head would stop spinning.

"Matthew Johnson isn't exactly a threat," she said defiantly, but he could hear the uncertainty behind the bravado. "And anyway, I can deal with him. You just stay here."

He wasn't any happier when she touched the handle of the holster of her gun as if to reassure herself.

"Do you have more weapons?" he demanded.

"Some. A couple of hunting rifles and a few more handguns."

"Bring me one. Please."

As much as it galled him to ask her, he knew he needed to conserve his strength.

"Do you know how to handle human weapons?"

"Yes. I am a warrior."

The knowledge emerged from his muddled brain with absolute certainty. She must have heard the conviction in his voice because she left the room, returning a moment later with a long barreled weapon. She handed it to him just as he heard a carriage come to a halt outside the house. She sighed.

"I don't think you'll need it, but I kind of like having you at my back."

She gave him a shy smile, and brushed her mouth across his before straightening her shoulders, marching out into the hallway, and throwing open the door. She stepped out onto the porch, but to his relief she left the door open so he could hear the conversation.

"You're not welcome here, Matthew," she said, her voice hard.

"Now is that any way to talk to your new neighbor?"

Harkan immediately hated the sound of the other male's voice. It had a slimy quality, as if it were wrapped in rotting jemmon weed. Using the weapon as a crutch, he managed to maneuver himself to his feet and quietly made his way to the entrance of the room.

"Thank goodness you're not my neighbor. Your foul stench would curdle the milk."

From this position he could see her body framed in the doorway and see the tension in her shoulders, but she managed a lazy, contemptuous drawl.

A horse neighed outside, and he caught her quickly hidden flinch.

"And if you don't stop sawing at those reins, you'll ruin that horse."

"I don't need your advice, missy." The male's voice was no longer quite so smooth. "And I'm delighted to tell you that we really are neighbors. The Carters just sold out."

This time, she wasn't as successful in hiding her reaction, and the male gave a self-satisfied laugh.

"Doesn't it make you feel better to know that you have a big strong man nearby? Available any time, day or... night."

The suggestive drawl in the last words was too much. He brought the weapon up to parade rest and strode across the hallway to stand next to his mate. His legs threatened to tremble, but his anger kept him upright.

"She doesn't need your assistance at any time. I am here to assist her."

He wanted to go further, to claim her as his mate, but this was not the place.

The male gaped at him in almost comical surprise. He was human—a big, older male, his muscles beginning to turn to fat but still a powerful adversary. The male's eyes narrowed as the shock wore off and he glared at Rosalie.

"You hired a fucking alien? Your husband must be rolling in his grave."

Husband?

The world whirled around him, and once again his knees threatened to give way. Somehow he managed to remain upright. His female—or was she his female?—had recovered her composure. She raised an eyebrow, her voice hard.

"I'm sure Hector would be delighted—especially since any man I try to hire mysteriously disappears."

The male leaned over and spat a gob of brown liquid into the dirt.

"On your head be it. You know folks around here don't take much to aliens."

"Since you appear to be the only folk left around here and I don't give a damn about your opinion, I'm not worried."

"Don't say I didn't warn you. Time is running out, missy."

The male spat again, then brought the reins down hard across the horse's back and disappeared back down the drive. Rosalie sighed and rubbed her forehead.

"It was nice of you to come to my defense, but it wasn't necessary. Damn. I can't believe the Carters sold their property to him. Their farm was the last buffer between us." She frowned up at him. "Is something wrong? I knew you shouldn't have gotten out of bed."

"You're already mated?" The words sounded strange in his ears.

"Mated? Do you mean married? Yes, I was married, but my husband died over a year ago."

He swayed again, and she immediately tucked herself under his arm. He knew the honorable thing to do would be to avoid her touch, but he was not strong enough. Instead, he tightened his arm around her shoulders, relishing his last chance to touch her.

"I apologize. I did not know."

"Of course you didn't know. We haven't had much chance to talk."

She looked up with a teasing smile and his chest ached. He had been so sure she was his mate.

"I would not have touched you if I had known."

By this time they had reached the bedroom, and she helped him down onto the bed before standing back, her hands going to her hips.

"What do you mean you wouldn't have touched me? I told you he's been dead for over a year. I'm not the unfaithful kind."

"But he was your mate." Even though the lingering sweetness of her arousal still filled the air.

Her foot tapped impatiently against the floor.

"Yes, we *were* married, but we're no longer married because he died. I don't understand why you're acting like this. You're the one who kissed me." Her mouth suddenly dropped open. "Oh my God. Are you being so weird because I'm not a virgin?"

As if he cared about how many sexual partners she'd had. He opened his mouth to explain that he was only concerned with her mating status, but she didn't give him a chance to speak.

"Damn men—"

"I am not a man."

"All right, damn aliens. So determined to be the first one to enter a woman no matter how many times they've gotten their own dick wet. As soon as you can walk, get the hell off my farm."

She turned and stomped through the doorway. He tried to rise and follow her but it was no use. Between the walk from the barn to the house and the confrontation on the porch, he simply had no strength left. No matter how much he hated it, he was going to have to recover his strength before he could go after her.

Recover my strength.

The words triggered another flash of memory and this time it didn't immediately disappear. He was sure he had come to Cresca for help, even if he didn't know how he'd intended to accomplish that. He still had no idea how he'd ended up on the farm. He liked this room, liked the tall ceiling and the big windows, but it was a home, not a medical establishment. More flashes of memory—of white walls and hard mattresses and people shaking their heads before they walked away. No one had been able to help him. Or had they? A doctor with a kind face had suggested a possibility. He could even remember that feeling of hope but no other details surfaced.

Fuck. It didn't matter anyway. All that mattered was his female. Even if she could never be his mate, he still intended to protect her. He just had to get his strength back first.

CHAPTER 5

Rosie gently detached the portable milking machine from Petunia's udder, then leaned against the cow's flank with a sigh. She knew she should take the milk to the dairy for processing, but instead her thoughts kept returning to Harkan, just as they had all day while she worked. Why couldn't she just dismiss him as another worthless male?

Petunia gave her a soulful look over her shoulder with her big brown eyes, aware that something was different and Rosie forced herself to sit up.

"Never mind, girl. I'm just being an idiot."

"You are not an idiot."

That deep voice sent a shiver of pleasure through her body, but she didn't look up.

"You seem to have made a remarkable recovery."

In spite of her annoyance, she had checked on him several times throughout the day and always found him sleeping. Each time she'd left him more water and broth but made no attempt to wake him.

"My... condition can recede as quickly as it appears."

That surprised her into frowning up at him.

"Does that mean you're well again?"

He did look better—tall and confident—but then she was pretty sure he had appeared confident to Matthew as well. She took a longer look, telling herself it was strictly for medical reasons, and not because she was appreciating that strong muscled body.

"No, I am not well," he said after a long hesitation. "The sickness will return."

Her heart skipped a beat.

"You mean you remember? Is that why you –"

"It's not important," he interrupted. "What is important is that I have distressed you and I did not intend to do so. I believe that I may have misunderstood."

He seems sincere enough. Perhaps it was a cultural misunderstanding rather than the misogyny she'd assumed. She pushed the milking machine back out of the stall and picked up the canister of milk. He immediately reached for the heavy container. She hesitated, then let him take it. The ease with which he carried it certainly made it seem as if he were fit again.

"All right," she said as they headed to the dairy. "Why don't you explain it to me?"

He followed her into the whitewashed dairy and watched as she poured the milk into the separator. Then she led him through the outer door to the bench behind the barn. This was one of her favorite places on the farm, and one of her favorite views. The sun was sinking into the horizon over the gently rolling landscape, the line of trees that followed the creek already dark and mysterious in the increasing dimness.

"All right," she said as she sat down. "I'm listening."

After the briefest pause, he sat next to her. She could feel the heat of his body against the length of her side and did the best she could to ignore how good—how right—it felt.

"Your word marriage translates to mate bond in my language," he said slowly. "But perhaps the translation is incorrect. Amongst my people a mate bond is for life. Once mated, a Riasi never looks at another female."

"Not even if their mate dies?"

"No. Occasionally a surviving mate might seek comfort from another, but it would never be a true bond. But perhaps your human marriage is not the same."

She sighed and leaned back against the bench as the sun sank below the hills, leaving only a glowing line of gold along the horizon.

"Yes and no. Usually a person marries with the intention that it will be for life, but it doesn't always work out that way."

"You said usually? Was this not true for you?"

She shook her head.

"I grew up here. My pa had a farm on the other side of that ridge over there. He wasn't much of a farmer and it wasn't much of a farm, but we did our best. Then my mother died." That ache never went away. "We had a bad winter three years ago, and she was never strong. That next spring Pa decided he'd had enough of farming and sold the farm to Matthew. He tried to sell me too."

"He did what?" he growled, and she could feel his anger reverberating against her side.

Pa hadn't put it quite like that, of course. He'd told her that Matthew was willing to take her on and she should be grateful.

"He told me I was part of the deal. I'm not even sure why Matthew was interested—convenience, maybe. Farming is a hard life, even if you're brought up with it, and there aren't many women around."

"Or perhaps—despicable though he may be—he is intelligent enough to realize that you are a beautiful, desirable female."

His eyes glowed silver as he looked at her and her breath caught. The memory of their earlier encounter sent a surge of arousal humming through her veins, but she wanted him to understand.

"I'm ashamed to say that I almost considered it."

She'd hated the idea, but she was also keenly aware that she didn't have many alternatives. All she knew was farm work and no one in their cluster had the resources to hire her. She'd been trying to gather the courage to go to Wainwright to look for work when Hector approached her.

"Then Hector came to see me. His wife had also been taken that winter, leaving him alone and childless. He wanted someone to inherit the farm."

She could still see Hector standing in their kitchen, a tall, lanky man with a careworn face, twisting his hat in his hands. His proposal had been awkward, but he'd been honest about why he was proposing and she respected that.

"It wasn't a love match. It was clear that he still loved his wife. I think maybe they had one of those mate bonds, but he wanted an heir and I needed an alternative to marrying Matthew."

"And your father?"

"Told me I was a fool but didn't stick around long enough to argue. Matthew bought the farm anyway, and as soon as Pa had the money, he left. Haven't seen him since."

Harkan sprang to his feet, pacing back and forth in the growing darkness.

"How could any worthy male do that to his daughter?"

"It's pretty obvious he wasn't a good man," she said, trying to keep the hurt out of her voice. Her pa had never been kind to her, but she hadn't realized until that day how little he valued her.

He stopped pacing and knelt in front of her, gathering her hands in his big warm ones.

"I am sorry that you did not have the parent you deserved." His voice deepened. "And the male you married, was he… worthy?"

"Worthy enough. We worked hard, but I was used to that. We managed to get along well enough." But despite the weekly ritual of their marital duties, he'd always seemed like a stranger to her. She had wondered if that would change eventually, but she'd never had a chance to find out.

"We've been married for just over a year when there was an accident with one of the farm machines. He was working on it, and it fell on top of him."

"I'm sorry," he said softly, tightening his grip on her hands. "Was it truly an accident?"

"I think so. I suspected Matthew at first, but Hector was alone and there hadn't been anyone else around. I wondered if maybe part of him just wanted to join his first wife."

It was the first time she'd ever voiced her suspicion aloud, but Harkan only nodded.

"That would not be uncommon amongst my people, although it is done openly." His eyes glowed as he looked at her. "I would follow my mate into death."

The warmth in his eyes was unmistakable and her cheeks heated, but she wasn't sure she was ready for that discussion. Instead, she jumped to her feet, pulling her hands free so she could brush non-existent dirt off the knees of her pants.

"Hopefully nobody's going to be following anybody into death," she said as lightly as possible, but she felt him freeze. When she looked up at him, he was staring out into the darkness.

"They aren't, are they?" she whispered.

CHAPTER 6

Harkan saw the horrified suspicion on Rosalie's face and realized he had revealed himself. He couldn't bring himself to answer her question, so instead he changed the subject.

"Is there any other work which needs to be done tonight?"

From her penetrating glance he suspected she wasn't fooled, but after a moment's hesitation she gave him a rueful smile.

"There is always more work to be done on a farm, but right now it's time for supper. Let's go back to the house."

As she walked along the path behind the farm buildings, he stayed a half-step behind, his senses alert for any sign of trouble. He disliked her earlier visitor even more now that he knew the male had attempted to purchase his female, but how much of a threat was he? Was it merely talk, or was there more to it?

"This male who wants your farm, how dangerous is he?" he asked as they entered the kitchen.

She hesitated a moment too long before answering.

"Not very. He's really just all talk."

"I suspect he is somewhat more than that if the thought crossed your mind that he was involved in your husband's accident," he said dryly. "Do you need assistance with the meal?"

"I'm just going to heat up some soup and make grilled cheese sandwiches, but thank you for asking."

"Of course. But you are avoiding the subject."

She raised an eyebrow at him. "The same way you did?"

When he nodded, she sighed, then pulled out a loaf of bread and began cutting it fiercely into slices.

"He's never been caught, but unfortunate accidents always seem to happen at the farms he has his eye on. Not that he would ever get his own hands dirty, but the men who work for him don't have many scruples."

"Have they happened here?" he asked.

"There have been a few things," she admitted, placing thick slabs of cheese between the slices of bread and adding them to a sizzling pan. "But they could all have been genuine accidents. The belts on farm equipment break and fences get damaged all the time."

"But you don't think they were accidents?"

"No, not really." Although she kept her attention focused on her cooking, her shoulders had stiffened again. "But they certainly aren't going to drive me off my land."

His chest ached. He had thought the same thing once, but now his home no longer existed. He vowed to find a way to make sure that she didn't suffer that same loss.

"I know that probably sounds strange considering how I came to be here," she added. "But I think when you work the land it becomes part of you. This feels like my home."

"I understand. My family also worked the land."

"You? A farmer?"

An infectious laugh bubbled out of her pretty lips, and he found himself smiling back. How long had it been since he'd smiled?

"I assure you I am quite capable," he said with mock offended dignity, and she laughed again as she served up their meal.

They carried the plates into the living room and ate in front of the fire. The dim overhead lights flickered and finally died, but she only sighed and lit the lantern she had ready.

"The solar generator is on its last legs but I can't blame that on Matthew. It's just old."

He almost offered to repair it, but as his strength had returned, so had most of his memory. He couldn't stay with her for long. Instead, he found himself telling her more about his family and his past, while she told him about her life and the mother she had clearly adored. They talked long into the night, and the house was dark and still around them when at last she looked over at him, her eyes a deep mysterious blue in the glow of the lantern.

"I want you to come to bed with me."

His cock jerked, but he sternly suppressed it. He was determined not to allow any more misunderstandings between them.

"It is time to rest," he agreed cautiously, and she smiled—a slow, seductive smile that was impossible to resist.

"Rest isn't what I had in mind. I mean, if you feel well enough—"

"I do."

He gave into the impulse that had been haunting him all evening and lifted her into his arms. Satisfaction filled him as the soft curves of her body settled into place against him. This was where she belonged. He carried her through into the bedroom, then placed her back on her feet.

"May I remove your clothing?"

Pink flushed her pretty face, but she nodded. He started with her shirt, slowly and carefully unfastening each button, her skin impossibly soft beneath his fingers as he worked his way down before gently pushing the shirt away. She shivered, her nipples like ripe berries crowning her lush breasts.

"Are you cold, little mate?"

"No," she whispered. "Just impatient."

Her hands went to her pants, but he covered them with his own.

"This is my privilege."

His own hands threatened to shake as he carefully unfastened her pants, then slid them down the soft curves of her legs, leaving her naked and glowing in the dim light.

"You are so beautiful."

He could see she didn't believe him, but she would eventually. At least...

"What's the matter, Harkan?"

"Nothing," he said quickly, pushing the unwelcome thoughts aside. There was still hope, after all.

"Is it my turn now?"

"If that is what you wish."

"It's definitely what I wish."

The touch of her hands on his skin was a delightful agony as she took her time removing his clothing, stroking each inch of skin she revealed and tormenting him by pressing small teasing kisses to his flesh. He held out as long as he could, but after the third time her fingers railed tantalizingly across the head of his cock, his patience vanished. He growled, toed off his boots, stripped away his jumpsuit, and lifted her onto the bed in a rush of movement. Once again their bodies were pressed together, but this time was nothing between them. Never had anything felt so right.

She looked up at him, her eyes wide and startled, then gave him that same seductive smile.

"You seem to be in a hurry."

"If you put a feast in front of a starving man, you cannot expect him to contain his hunger forever."

"Are you starving for me, Harkan?"

"Ravenous," he said and kissed her.

His kiss was equally hungry. He told himself to slow down, but she met him with identical passion and his attempt at restraint vanished. Their mouths met in a sensual duel as their hands explored, searching, caressing. He tugged hungrily at those impudent nipples before diving lower, breathing a prayer of thanks to the gods when he found her wet and ready.

And small. He tried to remind himself to be patient, to take his time and make sure she was ready, but she writhed restlessly beneath him. Her legs wrapped around his hips, pulling him closer as he inserted one finger, then another, into her delicious little cunt.

She cried out her own prayer to the gods as her channel tightened around him, hot and wet and silky, and his last shred of control vanished. He yanked his fingers free and replaced them with his cock, thrusting into her with one long, hard stroke. Taking her. Filling her. Claiming her.

CHAPTER 7

*O*h. My. God.

Rosie's mouth opened but no words came out, her body overwhelmed by the massive cock splitting her open. Her breath escaped in rapid pants as she tried to adjust, hovering on the knife edge between pleasure and pain.

Harkan raised his head to look at her, his eyes glittering silver, then froze.

"Are you well, my mate?"

"I... I..."

The capacity for speech escaped her, and his expression turned to panic. He immediately started to pull free, but she gasped and clamped her legs tighter around his hips.

"Wait! Just... just give me a minute."

"I should have taken more time to prepare you."

The burning stretch began to fade, replaced by an incredible fullness, and she managed a smile.

"I'm not sure anything could have prepared me for you."

She flexed her hips cautiously. *Mmm.* Definitely feeling better. She tightened her muscles experimentally, and he groaned.

"You are testing my control, Rosalie."

Despite his words, he remained rigid, his muscles taut with strain.

"Then maybe you should move a little."

He obeyed, pulling back just enough that the ridges laddering his cock brushed across a place inside her that sent fire streaking through her veins. She gasped again, and he stopped moving.

"Don't stop," she said quickly. "That was a good gasp."

His worried expression began to fade.

"Ah. Then let us seek more of those."

He pushed back in the inch he had withdrawn, and those ridges felt just as good sliding into her.

"You seem to approve," he murmured, his hand coming up to tug gently on a taut nipple. "Is this what you want?"

"God, yes."

He started to move, still slowly and carefully, but her apprehension had vanished. She urged him on, the slight lingering burn only adding to her pleasure as he thrust harder, faster. Shivers skated across her skin, every nerve alive and singing as she climbed higher and higher towards that elusive peak.

"Mine," he growled, and his teeth clamped down on her neck, sending her flying.

Stars danced in front of her eyes, her body shuddering helplessly as he grew impossibly thicker, a rush of hot liquid filling her already full channel as her climax rolled on and on and on until the tremors finally ceased. He collapsed down over her, his body surrounding hers. She hugged him back just as tightly until at last he rolled to his back, keeping her tucked firmly against his side.

I could stay like this forever, she thought sleepily, then shivered. She had an uneasy feeling that they didn't have forever.

"Are you cold, little mate?"

Mate. It was impossible, and yet it felt so right. Was that why she was having this sudden rush of panic?

"What's wrong with you?" she blurted out. "You remembered, didn't you?"

His muscles tensed, but then she felt him nod.

"I think so. It's still a little confused, but I remember most of it." His fingers stroked through her hair. "I was injured during the war."

"But the war has been over for seven years."

"I know."

He fell silent, and despite the nerves making her stomach clench, she waited patiently for him to continue.

"It was an experimental weapon," he said at last. "A chemical that attacks the circulatory system. It appears to go into remission, but it comes back and each time it is stronger."

"You have to see a doctor!" she cried, trying to sit up.

Instead he pulled her closer, settling her on top of him. He felt so big and strong that it was hard to believe he was sick.

"I have seen a doctor. Many doctors. I've been poked and prodded and jabbed and scanned, but none of them had a lasting answer."

"Oh, Harkan, no."

Tears hovered on her lashes, and he stroked her hair again.

"Don't worry, my mate. I think I may have found the answer at last. There is a medic here on Cresca, an Arkani named Drakkar, who may be able to help me."

"Is he one of the aliens—I mean the males—who live at the ranch close to Wainwright?" she asked eagerly.

"Yes. I was heading there when the last attack hit me."

"Then we need to go there, right now."

His face softened, his hand coming up to cup her cheek.

"You would leave your farm unprotected from that despicable male?"

"I... Yes," she said defiantly, but he shook his head.

"No, my mate. You must remain here."

"But you'll come back?"

"Nothing could keep me away from you."

Except death, she thought, but she couldn't bring herself to say it out loud. Instead, she smiled as convincingly as she could.

"When will you leave?"

"As soon as it is light."

She wanted to object, to argue for more time together, but it would be foolish to delay.

"In that case, we should make the most of tonight."

She reached between their bodies and trailed her fingers down his cock. It responded immediately, stiffening beneath her touch, and his eyes glittered.

"An excellent plan," he agreed, and kissed her.

He loved her so fiercely and so well that despite her determination not to miss a moment of their remaining time together, she eventually fell asleep.

When the sun finally woke her, she was alone.

CHAPTER 8

Two weeks.

It had been two weeks since Harkan had left, and every moment since then had seemed like an eternity to Rosie. She tried to keep herself busy, but no matter how hard she worked she couldn't stop worrying about him. She barely slept, and what sleep she did get was haunted by nightmares.

Petunia mooed and nudged her, startling her out of staring unseeing at the milking machine.

"Sorry, girl," she apologized, and managed to focus long enough to complete the milking.

After taking the milk to the dairy she headed for the garden, deciding to harvest the last beans and can them. As she put her hand on the gate, the thuds of hooves disturbed the quiet. She looked up eagerly, her heart sinking as she recognized Matthew. This time he was not alone, two of his goons riding alongside him.

She checked the weapon on her hip and went to meet him.

"What do you want, Matthew? You know you're not welcome here."

She didn't bother to hide her contempt, and he sneered at her.

"Looks like that alien pet of yours wore you out. You should take better care of yourself."

Ignoring the insult, she gave him her coldest stare.

"I am not remotely interested in your opinion. Why are you here?"

"Actually, Randolph tells me that your alien isn't here anymore. Got tired of you, did he?"

That stung a little more than she liked. It had crossed her mind a few times, especially this week, that maybe Harkan had simply moved on, but she refused to believe it.

"No, he didn't," she said flatly.

Matthew actually looked surprised by her certainty, but then he sat back on his horse and smirked at her.

"Poor delusional woman. Hankering after some theoretical alien that's nowhere in sight. Sounds like you might be losing your grip on reality. Isn't that right, Randolph?"

"Losing her grip," the goon agreed, and the hair on the back of her neck stood up. What were they up to?

"Like I said, I don't care what you think. Move on."

"Oh, but you should care."

Matthew swung down from his horse, and she immediately pulled her gun.

"Stay right there."

"Now is that any way to talk to your future husband? Especially when he's the only one who's prepared to care for you in your uncertain mental condition?"

She stared at him in shock as ice streaked down her spine.

"What are you talking about?"

"I had a very interesting conversation with old Doc Martin. He agreed that you sounded unstable."

"That old drunk?" Doc Martin had been the town doctor before alcohol got the better of him. "I don't care what he thinks either."

"You should. He's prepared to testify that you need protective custody. And as your future husband, I should be the one to provide it."

She was so horrified by his plan that she almost missed the fact that both of his men had also dismounted and were moving to flank her. Refusing to panic, she pointed her gun at Matthew.

"If anyone gets one step closer to me, I'm going to shoot you."

His smug smile faded for a moment, but quickly reappeared.

"You forget that there's three of us. You can't shoot us all."

"Maybe not. But I can make sure you're the first to die."

He laughed unpleasantly.

"I wouldn't recommend it. Randolph and Duke are far less… civilized than I am when it comes to women."

Flicking a glance at the two leering men, she didn't doubt him for an instant, but she refused to be intimidated. She bared her teeth at him.

"I'll take my chances."

"Get her," he snarled, stepping back.

His men rushed her as she fired, one of them nudging her elbow enough that her bullet went through Matthew's arm instead of his chest. She whirled around to fire at Randolph, but he was no longer there. He was dangling from the claws of a huge winged alien. An equally large leonine alien with dark pink fur shoved Duke's face into the dirt. Ignoring the man squirming beneath his foot, he swept her an extravagant bow and grinned at her.

"You must be Rosalie. Nice to meet you."

"You too," she said automatically, before a strangled noise made her look back at Matthew.

He was suspended in the air with Harkan's hands wrapped around his neck.

"You're back!"

"I told you I would return, my mate." He smiled at her and she could already see how much healthier and stronger he looked. "I'm only sorry I was not in time to prevent this annoyance. But that can be easily remedied."

"No, wait!" she cried as his hands tightened, and he frowned at her.

"You are concerned for him?"

"Of course not, but I am concerned about you. All of you," she added. "The people who live around here have only just begun to accept other species. If you kill him, I'm afraid they'll turn on you."

"A valid point," the winged alien agreed as he landed next to her, his claws casually pressed against Randolph's jugular.

"You mean I can't pull his legs off?" the furred one asked, winking at her as the man under his foot moaned.

"I'm afraid not. Not this time. Of course, if they try to come back..."

"We won't," both men swore at the same time.

She gave Harkan a hopeful look. He sighed and nodded.

"All right. Disarm them and let them go."

The men glared at them as they were set free, but they kept their mouths shut, mounting rapidly and galloping away.

"Now you, Harkan."

"I don't like this," he scowled.

"I know. But do it anyway. Please."

"How can I refuse you, my mate?" Harkan lifted the gasping, red-faced Matthew higher. "From now on you stay away from my mate and from this place, do you hear me? Because if you step one foot onto this land, I'm going to let Benjar eat you."

The leonine male opened his mouth to reveal a truly impressive set of teeth, and Matthew shuddered.

"Now get out of here. Without saying another word," Harkan added as he dropped Matthew and Matthew's mouth opened.

The big man gave them all a death glare, but he obeyed. As soon as he was riding away, she flung herself into Harkan's arms and burst into tears.

"Hush, little mate. Everything is fine."

"I was so afraid you weren't coming b-back," she sobbed.

"I will always return to you, Rosalie. I love you."

That made her sob even harder, and he hugged her close.

"It's all right, sweetheart. I can wait until—"

"I l-love you too."

The words were muffled by her sobs, but he must have heard them because he grinned, and then he kissed her and everything else ceased to matter. He was home.

EPILOGUE

wo months later...

Harkan poked his head cautiously around the door of Petunia's stall, not surprised when Rosalie looked up and glared at him.

"So you're finally back from your mysterious errand?"

Despite the annoyance in her voice, he could also see the worry in her eyes and he bent to give her an apologetic kiss. For a moment she didn't respond, then she sighed and returned the kiss with her usual sweetness. His ever ready cock immediately began to stiffen and when she ended the kiss by nipping at his bottom lip, it grew even harder.

"I have missed you, my mate," he said, caressing her silky cheek.

"Then you shouldn't have left before I was awake without telling me where you were going." She held up her hand when he started to reply. "And a note telling me not to worry didn't help. All it did was make me think you were going to do something foolish."

He gave her a mock offended look.

"Me? Would I do something foolish?"

Her pretty lips twisted before she shook her head.

"All the time." She stood and put her hand on his arm, giving him an anxious look. "Is Matthew causing trouble again? I hoped he'd finally given up."

To no one's surprise, Matthew had not accepted his defeat graciously. Anticipating trouble, Drakkar and Benjar had helped Harkan set up monitors around the perimeter of the farm before they left. He had been able to respond quickly and effectively when anyone attempted to cross onto his mate's land. Reluctantly keeping her instructions in mind, he had not permanently injured anyone who approached, but he had made his feelings very clear. The attempts had slowly ceased as Matthew's hands found less threatening work.

He had hoped that the harassment would cease, and for a while it had as the remaining workers concentrated on the harvest. But Matthew had not been content to let it drop. A week after he'd reaped the benefits of the harvest and raised more capital, he recruited a new set of ruffians. Fortunately, the town rumor mill had been active enough that word of his intentions had reached the males on the ranch. Drakkar, Benjar, and several more of their brothers had come to his assistance. They had caught Matthew's gang trying to set fire to the woods at the edge of the farm—a fire that would have inevitably spread to their home. That time some of the human males disappeared for good.

However, as long as Matthew sat brooding on the farm next door, Harkan had no doubt that he would try again—and the next time he might not hear about it in time. He had conferred with Commander Artek, the leader of the aliens on the ranch, and together they had come up with a plan—a plan they had put in place today. He smiled down at Rosalie.

"No," he said reassuringly. "There was no problem with Matthew, and he will never cause trouble for us again."

Her brows drew together in an adorable frown. "Oh Lord, what did you do to him?"

"You are concerned for him?"

"Not at all, but I don't want you to get in trouble."

"I won't."

He reached into his pocket and pulled out the signed document he'd received—an actual paper document with an inked signature. Despite the primitive nature of the transaction, he'd been assured it was legally binding. He handed it to her and her eyes widened as she read it.

"I don't understand. Matthew sold his farm to you?"

"To us," he said immediately. "As my mate you have an equal share in everything I own."

"But why? How? And what are we going to do with it? We can't manage a farm that size. Why on Earth—"

He put a gentle finger over her soft lips.

"Can I explain?"

"I think you'd better." She sighed. "Perhaps we should go into the house first. I have a feeling I'll need some of that apple wine Artek's wife sent us."

Rosie's thoughts whirled as Harkan took the milk for processing while she settled Petunia for the night. He had taken to life on her farm with astonishing ease, even though the farm in his past had been much larger and more automated. He was helpful enough that she'd actually begun to consider expanding her dairy stock again and perhaps putting in another field of wheat, but those were modest increases compared to a farm the size of Matthew's.

She followed him silently into the house, but as soon as the door closed behind her, she put her hands on her hips and frowned at him.

"Well?"

He laughed and picked her up, swinging her around in a quick circle before settling onto one of the kitchen chairs with her nestled on his lap. Some of her tension disappeared in the comfort of the familiar position, and she sighed and settled into his arms. He too looked more relaxed. The faint indications of strain she'd seen on his face had vanished. He must have been more worried about Matthew than he'd let on.

"Now talk," she said, gently poking his big chest. "What happened to Matthew?"

"He should be just about ready to embark on a spaceship leaving from Port Cantor."

Her mouth dropped open.

"A *spaceship*? Why is he doing that?"

"Commander Artek, Benjar, and I went to see him. We made him an offer he was unable to refuse."

That certainly sounded ominous.

"You mean you threatened him?" she asked suspiciously.

"Not at all." His innocent look turned to a broad smile. "Although it's certainly possible that he may have been somewhat intimidated by the presence of the three of us in his study. He did seem to find Benjar's teeth rather alarming."

She couldn't help laughing as she pictured the moment, but she still shook her head.

"That sounds like a threat to me."

"Perhaps, but you know as well as I do that he is a very stubborn male. He would not have agreed to the sale without the financial compensation we offered him. Now he has a very large credit chit in his pocket, and he seems convinced that there are better worlds for him. Benjar kindly escorted him to the spaceport so he may find out."

She suspected it hadn't been quite as easy as he made it sound, but the relief of knowing Matthew was gone made it easy to overlook.

"I have to admit I'm happy he's leaving, but I still don't understand. Where did the credits come from?"

"They were mine. I received compensation from the government of Vizal for the destruction of my family's land." His mouth twisted. "I never had any intention of using it, but I changed my mind after I talked to Artek. Do you remember what I told you about the New Hope Ranch being purchased by Artek as a place for his brothers to heal from the war?"

"Of course." Her heart ached at the thought of what all of them had gone through.

"He had been wondering if other former warriors also needed help. We think Matthew's farm—our farm—could provide a refuge for those warriors. That is, if you are agreeable?"

Her eyes filled with tears.

"Of course I am. But how is this going to work?"

"Matthew's farm is composed of fourteen smaller farms. We thought we could teach anyone who comes here what needs to be done to be self-sufficient. When they are ready, we can section one of the smaller farms off to them. But they won't be alone—we will form a new community. What do you think?"

He looked so worried, but how could he possibly think she'd disapprove?

"I think it's a wonderful idea. And you're wonderful for thinking of it."

"Not me," he protested, but he was smiling now. "I believe Nelly was the one who came up with the idea originally."

"Of course she was."

She laughed, then sat upright, adjusting her position so that she was straddling him. The stiff ridge of his erection settled between her legs, exactly where she needed him, and a pleasant shiver trailed down her spine as she rocked gently against his shaft.

"I missed you today," she whispered.

"I missed you too."

His big hands settled on her hips, helping her move.

"And I was thinking—"

"Now?"

His wonderfully rough tongue lapped at her neck, sending little pulses of excitement to her clit.

"Yes, now." Her voice came out breathless, but she did her best to concentrate. "Maybe our new neighbors will find mates, and start families as well…"

His body stiffened as he raised his head.

"Families?"

"Yes. And if we're going to be showing them how to farm, maybe we should show them a happy family as well."

His eyes blazed silver, but his hands remained locked in place.

"Do you mean you want a child?"

"Yes. I love you, Harkan, and I want it all. A child. A family. That is, if you—"

His mouth crashed down over hers and in the five seconds before he had her naked and stretched out on the kitchen table, she decided he wanted it just as much. Then he buried himself inside her and all rational thought disappeared.

NINE MONTHS LATER…

"Our son," Rosie breathed, looking down at the baby in her arms.

He had her curly hair, but it was as dark as his father's with that same hint of emerald green. He had his father's silver eyes as well, but his skin was the same golden color as her own. He was perfect.

Harkan returned from escorting Drakkar to the door and sat next to her, stroking his finger down their son's cheek.

"Thank you," he whispered.

"Why are you thanking me?"

"Everything the war took away from me, you have returned in overflowing measure."

She put her hand over his and gave him a watery smile.

"And you have given me what I always wanted most, a real family."

He brushed his mouth across hers, then gathered her close as they both settled down to watch their son sleep.

AUTHOR'S NOTE

Thank you so much for reading **You Got Alien Trouble!** This is a shorter story than I usually write - written to a specific length for a podcast - but it was a delightful challenge to create a complete story within those boundaries. And, of course, I had to add an epilogue to give you a glimpse into the future!

Whether you enjoyed the story or not, it would mean the world to me if you left an honest review on Amazon – reviews are one of the best ways to help other readers find my books!

As usual, I have to thank my readers for coming on these adventures with me - I couldn't do it without you!

And, as always, a special thanks to my beta team – Janet S, Nancy V, and Kitty S. Your thoughts and comments are incredibly helpful!

If you enjoyed **You Got Alien Trouble!**, you're going to

AUTHOR'S NOTE

LOVE the *Seven Brides for Seven Alien Brothers* series beginning with ***Artek***!

A whirlwind courtship and a hasty marriage are only the beginning for Artek and Nelly. Can two people who know nothing about each other possibly find happiness together?

Artek is available on Amazon!

To make sure you don't miss out on any new releases, deals, or updates, please visit my website and sign up for my newsletter!

www.honeyphillips.com

OTHER TITLES

HOMESTEAD WORLDS

Seven Brides for Seven Alien Brothers

Artek

Benjar

Callum

Drakkar

Endark

Frantor

Gilmat

You Got Alien Trouble!

Cosmic Fairy Tales

Jackie and the Giant

Blind Date with an Alien

Her Alien Farmhand

KAISARIAN EMPIRE

The Alien Abduction Series

Anna and the Alien

Beth and the Barbarian

Cam and the Conqueror

Deb and the Demon

Ella and the Emperor

Faith and the Fighter

Greta and the Gargoyle

Hanna and the Hitman

Izzie and the Icebeast

Joan and the Juggernaut

Kate and the Kraken

Lily and the Lion

Mary and the Minotaur

Nancy and the Naga

Olivia and the Orc

Pandora and the Prisoner

Quinn and the Queller

Stranded with an Alien

Sinta - A SciFi Holiday Tail

Folsom Planet Blues

Alien Most Wanted: Caged Beast

Alien Most Wanted: Prison Mate

Alien Most Wanted: Mastermind

Alien Most Wanted: Unchained

Exposed to the Elements

The Naked Alien

The Bare Essentials

A Nude Attitude

The Buff Beast

The Strip Down

Horned Holidays

Krampus and the Crone

A Gift for Nicholas

A Kiss of Frost

Treasured by the Alien

Mama and the Alien Warrior

A Son for the Alien Warrior

Daughter of the Alien Warrior

A Family for the Alien Warrior

The Nanny and the Alien Warrior

A Home for the Alien Warrior

A Gift for the Alien Warrior

A Treasure for the Alien Warrior

Three Babies and the Alien Warrior

The Alien Invasion Series

Alien Selection

Alien Conquest

Alien Prisoner

Alien Breeder

Alien Alliance

Alien Hope

Alien Castaway

Alien Chief

Alien Ruler

COZY MONSTERS

Monster Between the Sheets

Extra Virgin Gargoyle

Without a Stitch

Sweet Monster Treats

Cupcakes for My Orc Enemy

Cyborgs on Mars

High Plains Cyborg

The Good, the Bad, and the Cyborg

A Fistful of Cyborg

A Few Cyborgs More

The Magnificent Cyborg

The Outlaw Cyborg

The Cyborg with No Name

ABOUT THE AUTHOR

USA Today bestselling author Honey Phillips writes steamy science fiction stories about hot alien warriors and the human women they can't resist. From abductions to invasions, the ride might be rough, but the end always satisfies.

Honey wrote and illustrated her first book at the tender age of five. Her writing has improved since then. Her drawing skills, unfortunately, have not. She loves writing, reading, traveling, cooking, and drinking champagne - not necessarily in that order.

Honey loves to hear from her wonderful readers! You can stalk her at any of the following locations...

www.facebook.com/HoneyPhillipsAuthor
www.bookbub.com/authors/honey-phillips
www.instagram.com/HoneyPhillipsAuthor
www.honeyphillips.com

Printed in Dunstable, United Kingdom

78135848R00048